GIRLS
Horsing Around

Jacqueline Arena

illustrated by
Monika Maddock

MACMILLAN

First published in 2005 by
MACMILLAN EDUCATION AUSTRALIA PTY LTD
627 Chapel Street, South Yarra 3141
Reprinted 2005, 2006

Visit our website at www.macmillan.com.au

Associated companies and representatives throughout the world.

National Library of Australia
Cataloguing-in-Publication data

Arena, Jacqueline.

  Horsing around.

  For primary school students.
  ISBN 978 0 7329 9883 7.
  ISBN 978 0 7329 9876 9 (Set 1).
  ISBN 0 7329 9883 2.
  ISBN 0 7329 9876 X (Set 1).

  1. Horses – Juvenile fiction. I. Title. (Series:
  Girlz rock!).

A823.4

Series created by Felice Arena and Phil Kettle
Project Management by Limelight Press Pty Ltd
Cover and text design by Lore Foye
Illustrations by Monika Maddock

Printed in Australia by McPherson's Printing Group

GIRLZ ROCK!
Contents

Jules   Rosa

CHAPTER 1

The Waiting Game

Best friends Jules and Rosa are
on their way to the farm to see
Jules's aunty.

Rosa "I can't wait to get there!"
Jules "I know. You've only said that
  about a million times now."

Rosa "I'm just so excited. I can't believe we're going horse riding. My first time!"

Jules "Yeah, well, I s'pose I was excited when I rode for the first time. But there's plenty of spare riding gear for us. Your mum didn't need to buy all that stuff, y'know."

Rosa is dressed from head to toe in horse-riding gear. She's wearing a helmet, riding pants and long riding boots.

Rosa "Oh well, when I get good at riding, I'll be happy I have my own gear. And besides, these boots are so cool."

Jules "Riding isn't easy. It takes a long time to get the hang of it."

Rosa "Yeah, well bring it on 'cause I'm ready—I can't wait! I've watched so many horse movies in the last week, 'Seabiscuit', 'Black Beauty', 'Spirit' ..."

Jules "Wow, you're obsessed, big time! You'll probably start off on something easy. Like sitting on top of a fence."

Rosa "No way!"

Jules "Yeah, way."

Rosa pulls out a book from her backpack.

Rosa "This is my book of horse jokes. Here's one. What did one horse say to the other horse in the next stable?"

Jules "What?"

Rosa "How are you doing there,
  neigh-bour?"

Jules (groaning) "Oh, that's so bad!
  You must be excited."

Rosa "I know. I am. I can't wait!"

Jules "Well, you don't have to wait
  anymore 'cause we're here."

CHAPTER 2

Horsey Heroes

Jules and Rosa hop out of the car and walk towards the stables with Jules's aunty.

Rosa "This is gonna be so cool. I can smell the horses from here. They totally stink but I don't care, I love it!"

Jules "I can put up with anything if it means I'll be riding soon."

Rosa and Jules open the stable door and head inside.

Rosa "Oh, wow! These horses look unreal. I couldn't pick between them, they're all so pretty,"

Jules "Okay, okay, before you fall in love with them *all*, come and I'll introduce you to the gang."

Jules "This grey one's called Jasper. Hi, Jasper, you beautiful boy. I always ride Jasper. He used to be a police horse."

Rosa "Cool! It'd be so great to ride a police horse and get paid for it!"

Jules "I know, wouldn't it!"

Rosa "Imagine if we were on our police horses and we saw a robber take an old lady's handbag."

Jules "Yeah, and then we'd chase after him."

Rosa "And we'd jump over rubbish bins and park benches."

Jules "Then we'd catch the robber by throwing a lasso around him!"

Rosa "And then we'd be heroes. And famous!"

Jules "Yeah, and people would say when they see us ride by: 'There go those cool police girls and their amazing horses!'"

Rosa "Yeah, that'd be awesome!
Wow, look at him. What's *his*
name?"

Jules "That's Lightning Dust, or
Dusty for short."

Rosa "I really like him. He looks so
proud, as if he owns the place.
Guess he must go like the wind
with a name like that."

CHAPTER 3

Dusty and Bucky

The girls move a bit closer to
Lightning Dust.

Rosa "Dusty's huge! Hi, Dusty."
Jules "Yeah, he was a champion
   racehorse. I think he even ran in
   the Melbourne Cup."

Rosa "Really?"

Jules "Yeah, really. It's one of the biggest horse races in the country."

Rosa "Oh, derr! I think it'd be unreal to be a jockey and ride horses all day. And to win a race like the Melbourne Cup would be totally brilliant."

Jules "Yeah, imagine if we were in the Melbourne Cup.

"And Rosa takes the lead, but look out, here comes Jules on ..."

Um, what would I call my horse?"

Rosa "How about Britney?"

Jules "Nah, we're not on the stage, y'know. It's gotta be something more speedy like Flash Bolt.

'And here comes Jules on Flash Bolt. They take the lead and yes! They win the Melbourne Cup!'"

Jules turns around to see that
Rosa has moved to the far end of the
stable to meet yet another horse.

Jules (shouting) "Be careful of him,
Rosa. He gets nervous with
strangers. He's a little jumpy."

Rosa "And what's *his* name?"

Jules "He's Bucky and he's a wild
boy. He used to be a bucking
horse in a rodeo."

Rosa "He doesn't look too wild
to me."

Rosa gently pats Bucky on the nose.

Jules "Wow, that's amazing. He must like you. He never usually lets people get close to him."

Rosa "See, I told you I love horses. I think being a cowgirl at a rodeo would be totally cool. I know I wouldn't get bucked off but if I did, I'd just land on ..."

Jules "Your butt?"

Rosa "No, on my feet, Smarty. So, d'you think I could ride Bucky?"

Jules "Don't think so. Not for your first time."

Rosa "What about Dusty, then?"

Jules "Nuh. He's my aunty's horse. No-one ever rides him except her."

Rosa "Then how about Jasper?"

Jules "He's mine."

Rosa: "Then which horse can
I ride?"

Jules "Maybe him—Brutus. He's a
Shetland pony."

CHAPTER 4

Pony Express

The girls make their way over to where Brutus is grazing.

Rosa "A pony?"

Jules "Yeah."

Rosa "But he's so small."

Jules "So, he's still fun to ride."

Jules opens the gate to Brutus's
pen. The girls walk in and pat
the pony.

Rosa "He's tiny. He only comes up
to my chest. Are you sure I can't
ride Dusty?"

Jules "Yeah, pretty sure. But why don't you just sit on Brutus and see what you think?"

Rosa "How do I get on his back?"

Jules "Just hold on to his mane to pull yourself up. That's it. How does that feel?"

Rosa "Wow, it's really high up here. But it feels good."

Jules (scoffs) "And you wanted to get on Bucky."

Rosa squeals and startles Brutus. Brutus bolts from his pen and gallops out the main gate—with Rosa on top!

Jules (shouting) "Hold on, Rosa!
  Hold on!"

Jules grabs a nearby bridle and runs
  after Brutus and Rosa.

Rosa (screaming) "ARRGGHH!!
  Jules, make him stop!"

CHAPTER 5

First-time Rider

Rosa holds onto Brutus for dear life
as he gallops wildly across the
paddock, disrupting everything
in sight.

Rosa "Woah, fella!"

Suddenly Brutus stops, throwing
Rosa off.

Jules "Rosa, Rosa, are you okay?"

Rosa "That was SO cool! I wanna do that again."

Jules "Are you sure you're okay?"

Rosa "Yeah, I'm lucky I landed in this grass. Whatever this padded thing under me is, it sure is soft."

Rosa stands up to find she has landed in horse poo.

Rosa and Jules "Eeeww! Gross!"

The girls collapse with laughter.

Jules "We'd better get Brutus back in his pen before anyone gets back. Come here, boy, I'll put your bridle on."

Rosa wipes her hands on the grass, then heads off with Jules and Brutus. She makes a squishing sound as she walks.

Rosa "There you go, Brutus, back in your pen. Sorry I scared you."

Jules grabs a wire brush and some old rags and helps Rosa clean the poo off her pants.

Rosa "This is the part of horse riding I don't like. Yuk!"

Jules "Just breathe through your mouth. There, I think most of it has gone."

Rosa "Thanks, Jules. All part of the lesson, I guess."

Just then, Jules's aunty returns. She asks Rosa if she's ready for her first ride.

Rosa (grinning at Jules) "Um, yeah, I can't wait."

As Rosa turns around, Jules's aunty sees her pants and gives Rosa a puzzled look.

Rosa "Those horses sure make a mess!"

Jules "Pity you fell over in the stables."

Rosa "Yeah, real pity! Now it's time for some good *clean* fun."

Then, with a wink, the girls get ready for Rosa's first (official) riding lesson.

GIRLZROCK!
Horse Lingo

Jules

Rosa

bolt When a horse suddenly takes off running.

bridle Straps that go around the horse's head for the reins and bit to attach to.

mane The long hair that runs along the top of the horse's neck.

stud A farm for breeding horses.

thoroughbred A racehorse bred from one pure breed.

GIRLZROCK!
Horse Must-dos

⭐ Always wear a helmet—but you can take if off when you're sitting in your mum's car.

⭐ Be calm when you're around horses. They can smell fear!

⭐ Wear good, solid boots. Imagine if a horse stood on your toes while you were wearing sandals—yeow!

⭐ Before patting a horse, let it sniff the palm of your hand. Keep your fingers flat and close together so that it can't bite at them.

⭐ Sing gently to horses. Country and western is their favourite music!

☆ Before you go riding try to get into the horse mood. Watch movies such as "Seabiscuit", "Spirit" or "Black Beauty".

☆ Breathe through your mouth if you step in horse poo or you might pass out if you get a whiff of it!

☆ If you're lucky enough to name a horse, call it something that describes its personality or the way it looks.

GIRLZROCK!
Horse Instant Info

The most horses ever to run in a horse race was 66. It was in a race called the Grand National in England, in 1929.

The prize for the richest horse race in the world is $6 million. It's the Dubai Cup in a country called the United Arab Emirates.

"Sire" is the name used for the father of a horse and "dam", for the mother.

The oldest recorded horse was an English barge horse called Old Billy. Old Billy lived to be 62 years old. The average life span of a horse is 20 to 25 years.

There are over 350 different breeds of horse.

Horses can walk, trot, canter and gallop.

A stallion is a male horse and a mare is a female horse.

A horse's feet are called hooves.

A person who cares for horse's hooves is called a blacksmith or farrier.

Many movies and television shows have been made about horses. Some of the famous ones are: "The Horse Whisperer", "My Friend Flicka", "Mr. Ed", and "National Velvet".

GIRLZROCK!
Think Tank

1 Seabiscuit is a cookie made out of seaweed. True or false?

2 What is the name of the oldest horse?

3 What piece of horse equipment does the word "bride" remind you of?

4 What type of music do horses love?

5 Name two things you should wear when you ride a horse.

6 What do Brutus, Jasper and Bucky have in common?

7 What do you use a horse's mane for?

8 What's a stud? (not the earring kind!)

Answers

8 A stud is a farm where horses are bred.

7 Riders grab onto the mane to help them onto the horse.

6 Brutus, Jasper and Bucky are all horses.

5 You should wear a helmet and a smile!

4 Horses love country and western music.

3 The word "bride" should remind you of "bridle".

2 The name of the oldest horse is Old Billy.

1 False. Seabiscuit was a famous racehorse. It's also the name of a film based on the great champion.

How did you score?

- If you got all 8 answers correct, you're horse-crazy! You probably have posters of horses stuck up on your bedroom wall (and if you haven't, you should).

- If you got 6 answers correct, you like horses and don't mind watching a great horse movie.

- If you got fewer than 4 answers correct, you'd rather ride your bike!

Hey Girls!

I hope that you have as much fun reading my story as I have had writing it. I loved reading and writing stories when I was young.

Here are some suggestions that might help you enjoy reading even more than you do now.

At school, why don't you use "Horsing Around" as a play and you and your friends can be the actors. Get a horse-riding helmet (a bike helmet will do), some high boots and a broom (as your horse) to use as props. So ... have you decided who is going to be Rosa and who is going to be Jules? And what about the narrator?

Now act out the story in front of your friends. I'm sure you'll have a great time!

You also might like to take this story home and get someone in your family to read it with you. Maybe they can take on a part in the story.

Whatever you choose to do, you can have as much fun with reading and writing as a polar bear in a freezer!

And remember, Girlz Rock!

Jacqueline Srena

GIRLZ ROCK!

When We Were Kids

Jacqueline   Holly

Jacqueline talked to Holly, another *Girlz Rock!* author

Jacqueline "Did you go horse riding when you were younger?"

Holly "Yeah, all the time. I'd always ride my horse around in circles."

Jacqueline "That sounds strange."

Holly "And sometimes I'd eat fairy floss at the same time."

Jacqueline "Now that's really strange!"

Holly "If I was really lucky, I'd hear music."

Jacqueline "We are talking about horse riding, right?"

Holly "Yeah, riding the merry-go-round at our local show!"

GIRLZROCK!
What a Laugh!

Q How much does it take to fall off a horse?

A A buck!

GiRLZ ROCK!

Read about the fun that girls have in these **GiRLZ ROCK!** titles:

Hair Scare

Diary Disaster

Netball Showdown

The Sleepover

Bowling Buddies

School Play Stars

Pool Pals

Horsing Around

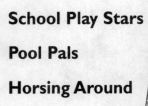

Girl Pirates

Surf Girls